Lucky O'Leprechaun in School

Lucky O'Leprechaun in School

Written and Illustrated by Jana Dillon

PELICAN PUBLISHING COMPANY
Gretna 2003

To William O. Hamby, with love

*The word "Pelican" and the depiction of a pelican are trademarks
of Pelican Publishing Company, Inc., and are registered
in the U.S. Patent and Trademark Office.*

Library of Congress Cataloging-in-Publication Data

Dillon, Jana.
   Lucky O'Leprechaun in school / written and illustrated by Jana Dillon.

      p. cm.
Summary: When Lucky O'Leprechaun goes to school, the students in Mr.
Eliot's class try to catch him and end up taking a trip to the moon.
   ISBN 1-58980-035-4 (alk. paper)
 [1. Leprechauns—Fiction. 2. Schools—Fiction. 3. Moon—Fiction.] I.
Title.
   PZ7.D5795 Lui 2003
   [E]—dc21

                   2002012061

Printed in China
Published by Pelican Publishing Company, Inc.
1000 Burmaster Street, Gretna, Louisiana 70053

LUCKY O'LEPRECHAUN IN SCHOOL

Sure'n the leprechaun trouble started the day B.B. cried, "Mr. Eliot, someone took bites out of Lydia's birthday cupcakes!"

"How rude," said Lydia. "Who would do a thing like that?"

'Tis true. Everyone in class knew each other. They knew no one would do that, except . . . maybe . . . the new boy?

Everyone looked at Kevin O'Malley.

"It wasn't me!" Kevin cried. "Look, the bite marks are tiny."

"True," said Mr. Eliot. "We believe you, uh, uh—" He looked at the class list. "Uh . . . Kevin."

Kevin O'Malley felt terrible, indeed. He had only been in school three days. No one here knew his name. No one here knew him at all. He was a nobody.

"Let's get back to your reports on the moon," said Mr.
Eliot. "They're due next week."
"The moon is a big boring rock," B.B. muttered.
The kids at her table giggled.

At snack time, B.B. wailed, "There are tiny teeth marks in my cookies!"

"Must be mice," said Mr. Eliot. "I'll set a trap with cheese after school."

Alas, the next morning, they found a pencil caught in the mousetrap and the cheese gone.

"Impossible!" said Mr. Eliot. "No mouse can outsmart a trap."

"Excuse me, Mr. Eliot," said Lydia. "I hear a tiny voice laughing at us from the closet!"

"A laughing mouse?" asked Mr. Eliot. "Couldn't be!"

Everyone grew silent as he yanked open the closet door. The closet was empty.

Suddenly, they heard tiny footsteps clattering above the ceiling.

"I hear shoes!" cried Mr. Eliot. "Mice don't wear shoes."

"Mr. Eliot," said Kevin, "my cousins, Meg and Sean, caught a leprechaun right in this neighborhood. His name is Lucky O'Leprechaun."

The kids began to snicker, but the footsteps overhead stopped.

"Sure'n aren't you the smarty-pants, Kevin O'Malley," sneered a little Irish voice from somewhere above the ceiling.

Everyone stared at Kevin. Now they knew Kevin O'Malley's name and would never forget it.

"If we can catch Lucky O'Leprechaun," whispered Kevin, "he'll grant us a wish."

"Begosh, I heard that, you little moneygrubber!" called Lucky O'Leprechaun.

"We'd better talk on the playground," said Kevin, "so he can't overhear."

Out on the playground, B.B. and Lydia stood guard, watching for a tricky little man in green, while Kevin explained about leprechauns: "If you see a leprechaun, you catch him by staring at him. He can't get away until he grants you a wish. But if you blink before you make your wish, he'll disappear, and you'll get nothing!"

"Oh, please, Mr. Eliot," said Lydia, "may we trap him?"

"Of course!" said Mr. Eliot. "But what shall we use for bait?"

"Snacks!" shouted B.B. "Snacks, snacks!"

"The cheese snack didn't work," said Kevin. "We need gold."

"Snaaacks!" bellowed B.B.

"*Gold,*" said Kevin.

"Kevin, we can't leave gold in school overnight," said Mr. Eliot. "Lucky might get away with it, like he got away with the cheese."

"*Snacks!*" hollered B.B.

"Hush, B.B.," said Lydia, shaking her head. "We need a compromise."

"I have an idea," said Kevin. "It's a snack and it's gold." He whispered his plan to the class and everyone cheered, even B.B.

"Now for the wish!" shouted B.B. "Gold! His pot of gold!"

"But, B.B.," said Kevin, "you know grownups. We can't ask for gold because all the adults in town would make us spend it their way."

"Sad," said Mr. Eliot, "but true. We'd lose control of it."

"Then let's ask for something no one can take away from us," said Lydia.

Everyone had a different idea. There was arguing and shouting. Then Kevin whispered his idea and the entire class began jumping up and down, chanting, "Ke-vin! Ke-vin!"

The next day, Mr. Eliot set an old cooking pot on his desk. Kevin opened a grocery bag and poured gold coins into the pot.

Mr. Eliot turned on a recording of Irish music. "Now, kids, it's time to dance an Irish jig. Except Kevin." Mr. Eliot winked. "Kevin, you hold the pot lid in the air and drum this wooden spoon on it so we won't lose the beat."

Soon the room was wild with Mr. Eliot and the students dancing. Kevin drummed up a loud racket.

Suddenly he slammed the lid down on the pot. "We got him!" Kevin shouted.

"Now, no blinking," warned Mr. Eliot. "Kevin, raise the lid."

Slowly, Kevin lifted the pot lid. And there was Lucky O'Leprechaun himself.

The little manny stamped his feet. "Sure'n what kind of phony gold is this?" He held up a gold coin and ripped off the foil. "'Tis mud inside!"

"Mr. Eliot," warned Lydia, "please, make our wish before he escapes!"

Lucky heard her. A sneaky smile curled his lips. "What's that behind you?" he cried.

Mr. Eliot and most of the kids twirled around to see, but nothing was there.

Kevin knew they'd better not wait one more second. "Our class wish, Lucky O'Leprechaun," Kevin said, "is that you take us on a field trip to the moon."

"The moon? No gold?" Lucky began to dance a jig. "They didn't ask for me pot of gold! Granted! Your wish is granted!"

The little fellow jumped onto the windowsill. "Take hold
of me coattails, Kevin boy-o, and everyone join hands."
Lucky O'Leprechaun flew out the window with the class
following him like a kite tail.

The children on the playground stopped playing and
stared after them.

As they flew higher and higher, the school got smaller and
smaller.

"There's my house!" shouted B.B. "Oh, my gosh! There's
the whole state! I mean, the whole country! I mean, the
whole world!"

Soon the kids were standing on the moon, looking back at the beautiful blue-and-white earth. With a wave of his hand, Lucky O'Leprechaun made every star visible. 'Twas awestruck into silence, they were.

Then, didn't they learn about the moon from the
leprechaun himself.
They wrote their names in moondust and collected
moonrocks.

Just before school dismissal time, Lucky gathered
them for the trip back to earth.
Begosh 'n' begorrah! It was a thrilling flight that
ended right in the classroom.

"Mr. O'Leprechaun," said Kevin, "you can keep the gold coins."

"Fine present, sport!" snapped the leprechaun. "'Tis foil and mud!"

"Taste one, please," said Lydia.

Lucky sniffed a coin. He took a bite. "It's sweet. It's delicious! It's—"

"Chocolate!" shouted the children.

Lucky grinned and bowed. "Ta. I'll be off now." Suddenly
he and the chocolate coins disappeared.
    But the children heard the crinkling of foil coming from
above the ceiling all the next week. And when it grew quiet,
they brought him some more.